I Can Read!

The Berenstain Bears'
KITTEN RESCUE

By Jan and Mike Berenstain

GOOD DEED SCOUTS

Living Lights™

ZONDERVAN.com/
AUTHORTRACKER
follow your favorite authors

ZONDERkidz

"Are we ready for our good deed
of the day?" asked Scout Brother.
"What shall it be?" asked Scout Sister.
"How about …" began Scout Fred.

Dear Parent:
Your child's love of reading starts here!

Every child learns to read in a different way and at his or her own speed. You can help your young reader improve and become more confident by encouraging his or her own interests and abilities. You can also guide your child's spiritual development by reading stories with biblical values and Bible stories, like I Can Read! books published by Zonderkidz. From books your child reads with you to the first books he or she reads alone, there are I Can Read! books for every stage of reading:

SHARED READING
Basic language, word repetition, and whimsical illustrations, ideal for sharing with your emergent reader.

BEGINNING READING
Short sentences, familiar words, and simple concepts for children eager to read on their own.

READING WITH HELP
Engaging stories, longer sentences, and language play for developing readers.

READING ALONE
Complex plots, challenging vocabulary, and high-interest topics for the independent reader.

ADVANCED READING
Short paragraphs, chapters, and exciting themes for the perfect bridge to chapter books.

I Can Read! books have introduced children to the joy of reading since 1957. Featuring award-winning authors and illustrators and a fabulous cast of beloved characters, I Can Read! books set the standard for beginning readers.

A lifetime of discovery begins with the magical words **"I Can Read!"**

Visit www.icanread.com for information on enriching your child's reading experience.
Visit www.zonderkidz.com for more Zonderkidz I Can Read! titles.

"Rescue the weak and the needy."
—*Psalm 82:4*

ZONDERKIDZ

The Berenstain Bears'™ Kitten Rescue
Copyright © 2010 by Berenstain Publishing, Inc.
Illustrations © 2010 by Berenstain Publishing, Inc.

Requests for information should be addressed to:
Zonderkidz, *Grand Rapids, Michigan 49530*

Library of Congress Cataloging-in-Publication Data

Berenstain, Jan, 1923 –
    The Berenstain Bears' Kitten Rescue / written by Jan and Mike Berenstain.
       p. cm. – (I can read. Level 1)
    ISBN 978-0310-72097-3 (softcover)
    [1. Cats—Fiction. 2. Animals—Infancy—Fiction. 3. Animal rescue—Fiction. 4. Bears—
Fiction. 5. Christian life—Fiction.] I. Berenstain, Michael. II. The Berenstain Bears Kitten
Rescue. III. Kitten rescue
    PZ7. B44826Bhk 2011
    [E]—dc22   2010016487

Editor: Mary Hassinger
Art direction & cover design: Jody Langley

Printed in China

14 15 16 17 /DSC/ 10 9 8 7 6 5

"Wait a minute," said Scout Lizzy.

"I hear something."

There was a soft, "Mew! Mew!"

"Look!" said Lizzy.

"A kitten is stuck in that tree."

"We will get it down," said Brother.

"That will be our good deed!"

"As the Bible says," Fred pointed out,

"'Whoever is kind to the needy

honors God.'"

"Good point, Fred," said Brother.

"How will we get it down?" asked Lizzy.

"I will stand on your shoulders,"

said Brother.

Then Scouts Sister, Lizzy, and Fred

stood on each other's shoulders.

Brother climbed up.

But he lost his balance.

They all fell down!

"Now what?" asked Sister

from the bottom of the pile.

"We need a ladder," said Brother.

"Maybe Papa can help."

Brother and Sister ran home.

Papa Bear was glad to help.

They carried the ladder to the tree.

"I want you cubs safe," Papa said.

"You hold the ladder.

I'll climb up."

Papa climbed up the shaky ladder and
out on a branch.
When the kitten saw Papa,
it got scared. It climbed higher.
Papa could not reach it.

"We need help," said Papa.

"Brother and Sister, go get

the fire department."

"The fire department?" cried the scouts.

"Hooray!"

14

Brother and Sister ran to the firehouse.
They told the fire-bears about
the kitten up the tree.

The fire-bears sounded the alarm.

They put on their gear.

They climbed onto their fire truck.

Brother and Sister climbed on too.

Lights flashed! Sirens blew!

The fire truck roared across town!

The fire truck pulled up to the tree.

A crowd gathered to see what

was going on.

A news van came to take pictures.

The fire-bears raised their ladder

to reach the kitten.

The fire-bears climbed up.

But the lights and the siren

scared the kitten even more.

It climbed to the top of the tree.

Not even the fire-bears' long ladder

could reach the kitten.

A long, fancy car pulled up.

It was the mayor.

"What's going on?" he asked.

"It's a kitten up a tree, Mayor,"
said the fire chief.

"But we need help.

We need the rescue copter."

The fire chief got on his radio.

He called the rescue copter.

Soon, the copter flew in.

It lowered a rescue bear

on a long rope.

He tried to reach the kitten.

But the rescue copter scared it.

The kitten hid in the leaves.

Mama Bear came by with Honey Bear.

They were coming from the store.

"Mama!" said Sister.

"Did you get any cat food?"

"Yes," said Mama. "I got it for
our kitten, Gracie."

"May I have it, please?" Sister asked.

Sister opened the cat food.

"Here, kitty, kitty!" she called.

The kitten peeked out of the leaves.

"Mew?" it said.

It climbed
right down to
eat the food.

"Hooray!" yelled
the crowd.

A lady ran out of the crowd.

"My kitten, Muffy!" she cried.

"Thank you so much

for saving her!

'I give thanks to the Lord, for he is good!'"

Everyone posed with the kitten.

The news bears took pictures.

Everyone was very proud

of the Good Deed Scouts.

Later, the Bear family watched the news.

They cheered when they

saw themselves on TV.

And they were very happy

that the kitten up a tree

was safe and sound.